The G Player of Zob

Written by Paul Shipton

Illustrated by Jan McCafferty

Collins

1 A rainy afternoon

The children had been playing a board game for fifteen minutes before they argued. Usually, it only took them ten minutes.

"A three! My hand slipped," said Jack. "I'll roll the dice again!"

"No! Stop cheating!" said Miles.

"Let's just play on," said Kate, who often tried to keep the peace between her older brothers. As usual, it was no good.

"YOU'RE the cheat!" cried Jack. "You moved forwards an extra space on your last go. I saw you!"

"Did not!"

Mum's voice echoed crossly down the stairs. "Children! Will you PLEASE stop arguing!"

Kate could hear that she wasn't just asking politely. She meant it.

It was the school holidays, but Mum was finishing some work in her office upstairs.

"I wish it would stop raining," sighed Kate. She looked outside hopefully and gasped …

A large, silver object was hovering in the air above the soggy lawn. It was clear what it was.

"A spaceship!" cried Kate.

"Don't be so si –" began Jack. He was going to say "silly", but he didn't get it out because then he too saw the spaceship.

All three children stared through the rain-streaked window in astonishment.

It was the most amazing thing they had ever seen ... until a few seconds later, when there was a flash of light and a loud crashing sound.

Suddenly, a strange-looking figure was standing in front of them in the room. Its body was human-shaped – two arms, two legs, one head – but its purple face looked like an octopus, with perhaps a bit of bat thrown in.

2 The Games Player of Zob

"Greetings, feeble earthlings!" the creature boomed at them.

As he was the oldest, Miles felt that it was his job
to speak to the newcomer.

"Are you from another planet, then?"

"Well, he's not from Earth, is he?" muttered Jack.

"Silence!" commanded the alien. "I am Vingor – the Games Player of Zob."

Kate tried a friendly smile. "That's nice. So – you like games, do you?"

"Do I like games?" The alien made a barking noise, which may have been a laugh. "I travel the galaxy in search of games to play. This is my first visit to this little planet and now I challenge one of you to a game. If you win, I will depart from your planet in peace."

Jack shrugged. "OK," he said.

But Kate knew something was wrong.

"What happens if we lose the game?" she asked.

Vingor made more of his unpleasant barking noises and patted something that hung from his belt. It looked dangerous.

"If you lose, I will zap you, of course. Isn't that what happens when you feeble earthlings play games?"

"What if we don't play?" said Miles.

"Then I will zap you," answered Vingor, matter-of-factly.
"If you quit, I will zap you. If you cheat, I will ..."

"Zap us?" guessed Kate.

"Correct!" beamed Vingor.

Miles pushed his glasses up his nose. "I think we'd better
tell Mum," he said, at last. Then he shouted: "Mum!"

Mum's voice sounded down the stairs.
"What is it? You three aren't
arguing again, are you?"

"Do not tell your parent-unit
anything," hissed Vingor.
"If you do, I will ..."

"Yes, we know," interrupted Jack. "Zap us."

Miles shouted up the stairs to Mum. "No, we're not arguing. We're ... just playing a game."

The three children swapped worried glances. It seemed there was only one way to avoid getting zapped.

Miles took a deep breath and pointed to the TV, where two controllers were plugged into a games console.

"OK, I'm the best in our family at *Wheels of Doom*," he said glumly. "I suppose we can play that."

3 Let the games begin

The two other children sat in nervous silence as the game began.

Wheels of Doom was a car racing game. Each player controlled a car and they raced two laps around a track on the screen. Miles tried to explain how to work the games controller, but Vingor seemed more than confident that he could do it.

"This is easy!" he barked, scornfully. "A monkey from Planet Gamma could play this! On my planet, we play *Spaceships of Doom*. That is much, much harder."

Miles gripped his controller, thumb at the ready.
"OK. Press "A" when you're ready. Are you ready?"

The alien nodded his head. There was a countdown on
the screen and then a black and white flag waved.
The cars set off. Instantly, Miles' car zipped into the lead.

"Wait!" cried Vingor. "I wasn't ready!"

He wasn't ready the next time either.

Or the next.

After three more false starts, the race was under way. It soon became clear that Vingor was not very good at *Wheels of Doom*. His car kept going off the track and spinning out of control.

For part of the race it went backwards. Then it went in the wrong direction. At one point it flipped completely upside-down.

"This is a stupid game!" complained Vingor, bitterly. "How can I be expected to play this?"

But Miles wasn't listening to Vingor moaning. He was concentrating on the screen. A few minutes later, his car crossed the finish line.

He looked across at Vingor, who was jabbing at his controller crossly with a finger.

Miles smiled. "I won!"

Jack was grinning, too.
"So that means you'd better
be going," he said to Vingor.

4 The best of three

However, there was a problem – the Games Player
of Zob was a bad loser.

"It's not fair!" he snapped. "My controller wasn't
working properly. Your Earth technology is rubbish!"
He threw the controller down in disgust.

It was clear that, although he had lost, Vingor wasn't
going anywhere. "We'll play the best of three!" he snarled.
"What's the next game?"

"That's not what you said before," protested Kate.

Vingor scowled.

"Everyone in the galaxy knows that a games challenge is the best of three," he said. He jabbed a purple finger in Jack's direction. "You, the one with the mouth hanging open – pick another game!"

Jack closed his mouth and looked around the room. His eyes fell on the table football. Yes! Nobody ever beat him at that. Jack slowly walked across the room and stood at one side of the table.

"We'll play this," he said.

"Perfect!" cried Vingor, looking at the game quickly. "On my planet, I am a champion *Spurgball* player – and we play with live Spurgs! With my superior speed and skill, I will crush you like a Blargian fly! My victory will be swift and wonderful!"

Vingor walked confidently to the table. However, when the first ball was put into play, Jack scored immediately.

"That goal doesn't count," said Vingor. "I wasn't ready."

The ball went into play once more. Jack scored again.

"You're cheating!" cried Vingor.

"I am not!" said Jack, furiously.

"You MUST be – how else could you beat the Games
Player of Zob?" hissed Vingor.

The alien's hand moved towards his zapper.
"Besides, it's not fair – the gravity on this stupid little
mud ball of a planet is giving me a headache,"
he whined. "I'm not going on with this game!"

The alien's voice had become louder and louder – so loud that Mum shouted down the stairs again.

"Whatever is going on?" she cried. "It sounds as if aliens are invading the planet or something! You know I'm trying to get some work done. Can't you play quietly?"

"Yes, Mum," answered all three children.
If only Mum knew how true her words were.
But they didn't dare tell her – not
with Vingor's hand
on the zapper.

Mum went back to work, muttering crossly to herself.

Still upset about the table football, the alien was glaring at Jack. "We'll play a *proper* game instead – a game from my home planet."

He tapped his chin thoughtfully. "I've got it! We'll play *Hunt the Snorkle Beast*."

"What's that?" asked Jack, nervously. He didn't much like the sound of this new game.

The alien's yellow eyes glittered. "*Hunt the Snorkle Beast* is an ancient game on my planet. Here's how you play it. I count to forty with my eyes closed, while you run away and hide. Then I look for you. When I find you – and I WILL find you – I zap you and I'm declared the winner!"

Jack nodded slowly. "We have that game, too, but it's got a different name on our planet and we don't zap people when we find them."

Jack didn't sound too worried. After all, he had played a lot of games of *Hide and Seek* in this house over the years. He knew all the good hiding places.

But Vingor was looking around.

"However, we will *not* play in this place, which is rubbish and clearly not good enough for a proper game of *Hunt the Snorkle Beas*t."

"No, we'll play the game on my spaceship."

Before Jack could protest, the alien
pressed a button on his belt and
there was a tremendous flash
of light. The next instant,
he was gone …

And so was Jack.

5 The chase is on

"Mum!" shouted Kate. "Quick! Come here!"

Mum did not sound happy. "What is it?" she said, coming down the stairs. "And this had better be important."

"Well …" Miles took a deep breath. "Jack has been kidnapped by an alien who wants him to play *Hide and Seek*."

Mum looked cross. "So let me get this straight … you've interrupted my work because you're playing a silly make-believe game about aliens? Well, I –"

She stopped.

She was looking out of the window at the spaceship hovering above the back garden.

"Erm, what's that?" Mum whispered. "Is there a giant balloon in our garden?"

"You'd better sit down, Mum," said Kate.

But before the children could explain anything to her, there was another brilliant flash of light in the room.

The flash of light was followed by another loud crashing sound.

Suddenly, a new strange-looking alien was glaring at them.

Mum didn't sit down – she fell to the floor in a faint.

This alien was even bigger than the first. "I am Plonga," she said. "Quick! I must find the one named Vingor."

Miles pointed a shaking finger at the spaceship in the garden. "He's out there."

"And so is our brother!" added Kate, urgently.

The two children quickly explained what was going on.

"If he finds Jack, he's going to zap him," said Kate. "You've got to stop Vingor!"

"I'm afraid it's not so easy," answered Plonga. "The ship's security system is switched on. It won't let me come on board unless Vingor tells it to."

She paused and looked at the children. "Unless … perhaps the security system won't be programmed to stop a human …"

"Send me!" said Miles quickly, but Plonga shook her purple head.

"You're too tall. The system will detect you and then it will stop you, too. No, we need a smaller human."

She looked down at Kate, who was listening carefully to all this.

"Well?" asked Plonga. "Do you think you can do it?"

Kate's answer was a quick nod.

6 Hunt the Snorkle Beast

Meanwhile, on the spaceship, things weren't going well for Jack.

As soon as Jack and Vingor arrived, the Games Player of Zob covered his eyes with both hands. He began counting, "One, two, three ..."

Jack would have been excited to be on a spaceship if he wasn't about to be zapped. Instead, he looked around frantically for somewhere to hide.

Jack was in a circular room which looked just as you might expect an alien spaceship to look – lots of flashing lights and buttons you shouldn't press (if you were sensible, that is).

There didn't seem to be any good hiding places, but there was a door on the other side of the room.

... 7, 8, 9...

Jack raced through this into a grey corridor.

Behind him, he could hear Vingor counting.
"Fourteen, fifteen ..." There was a pause, then:
"Thirty, thirty-one ..." That cheating alien had
skipped some numbers! But Jack knew there was
no point in protesting.

... 30, 31, 32...

He ran along the grey corridor and then into another
room. He hoped he would find somewhere to hide
in there.

To Jack's surprise, there was an
orange sofa in the room. You
might not expect to find a sofa
in a spaceship, but even
aliens need to sit down.

Jack ran behind the sofa and
crouched down. He tried to make
himself as small as possible in the
hope that the alien wouldn't be able to spot him.

In the distance he heard Vingor's gleeful shout:
"Ready or not, here I come, Snorkle Beast!"

 # 7 Zapped!

Jack waited, worrying whether he'd picked a good hiding place. It didn't really matter now though – it was too late to move to a different one. He waited some more.

Soon Jack started to get pins and needles in his leg, but he didn't dare stand up. What if Vingor heard him?

He stayed crouched behind the sofa and tried gently to rub his leg.

Suddenly, Jack heard footsteps in the doorway of the room.
"Are you in here?" called Vingor's voice happily from
the doorway.

Jack tried to make himself shrink even smaller.
He held his breath as the alien's footsteps came closer.

Maybe, just maybe, he could get away with it. But then …

"THERE you are!" cried Vingor. "I can see all that silly human hair on top of your head!"

That was it – the game was over. Miserably, Jack peeked out.

Vingor was holding the zapper and grinning down at him.

Jack's heart sank. He knew what was coming next – he was going to get zapped! But then Jack's heart leapt with relief.

There was someone else in the room behind the alien.

It was his little sister Kate!

Vingor was too excited to notice anything as Kate
tip-toed up behind him and then leapt forwards.

"Give me that!" cried Kate.

She grabbed the zapper right out of the alien's purple hands.

"Hey! That's mine!" cried Vingor. "Give it back!"

The alien lunged for the weapon, but Kate had always been good at another Earth game – basketball.
She threw the zapper over the alien's waving arms.

Jack jumped up and caught it.

Vingor turned and made a dive for Jack. The boy tried to throw the zapper back to his sister, but unfortunately he wasn't quick enough. Vingor was good at *Zekball* on his own planet and his hands wrapped around the zapper.

Alien and human wrestled desperately for control of the zapper. Then Jack grabbed hold of it and …

ZAP!

The zapper went off, shooting a jet of yucky green slime all over Vingor.

Jack took a step back.

Both he and Kate looked at the slime-covered alien in amazement.

"Is that all the zapper does?" asked Jack in surprise.

"Yes," replied Vingor, sulkily. "What did you think it did?"

 8 A very naughty boy

Miles and Plonga sat and waited in the house. The ticking of the clock sounded much louder than usual.

Miles cleared his throat. "So ... is Vingor a dangerous criminal? Is he on the run across the galaxy?"

Plonga stared at him. "Don't be silly! He's a very naughty boy and when I get him home, he's going to be sent straight to bed without any Skrull Pudding."

Miles was confused. "So you're not a police officer on your planet, then?"

"Of course not!" answered Plonga, impatiently. "I'm the babysitter. I look after Vingor every Blogsday."

Miles was struggling to understand this news.

Then, suddenly, there was yet another flash of light and a loud crashing sound, and Jack and Kate were back in the house once more.

Vingor was with them too, but he was no longer boasting. He had wiped off most of the gunk, but he was still looking very glum.

As soon as he saw Plonga, he knew he was in big trouble. The babysitter gave him a stern look. "How many times have I told you not to run off in your mum's spaceship?" she demanded.

"Three thousand, two hundred," mumbled Vingor, not meeting Plonga's angry eyes, "and eleven."

Plonga sniffed. "And what do you say to the nice Earth-children?" she said.

Vingor raised his eyes from the floor to look into the children's faces. "Thanks for playing with me," he mumbled.

"Er, that's OK," answered Jack. It seemed like the polite thing to say.

"Next time, why don't you let us know you're coming?" said Kate with a smile. "And we'll think of some really good Earth games to play."

A grin flashed across Vingor's face and he nodded.

Then the two aliens disappeared in a flash of light, but not before Mum woke up and saw them. She blinked, uncertainly.

"I'm seeing things," she mumbled, "I must have been working too hard."

"You're right," grinned Jack. "Why not have a break and play a game with us? We promise not to zap you!"

Earth games and Zob games

Ideas for reading

Written by Clare Dowdall BA(Ed), MA(Ed)
Lecturer and Primary Literacy Consultant

Learning objectives: understand how settings influence events, incidents and characters' behaviour; understand how expressive and descriptive language can create moods, describe emotions etc.; use phonic/spelling knowledge and graphic, grammatical and context cues when reading unfamiliar words; develop scripts based on improvisation

Curriculum links: Citizenship: Choices

Interest words: astonishment, feeble earthlings, newcomer, galaxy, matter-of-factly, parent-unit, Planet Gamma, Earth technology, gravity, security system, criminal

Resources: pens and paper

Getting started

This book can be read over two or more guided reading sessions.

- Introduce the book as a science fiction story and ask the children to share what they know about science fiction. What sort of settings and characters may be involved? Draw on their experience of films, television, games and storybooks.

- Read the blurb together. Ask them what they do on rainy afternoons in the holidays and how they feel and behave in these settings.

- Read chapter 1 together. Ask them to predict what is going to happen next after the alien appears.

- Ask them to think about the setting for the story. How does the setting affect the story? Is it believable? How could different settings make the story more or less scary or believable?

Reading and responding

- Read chapter 2 around the group. Model how to use a range of cues to decode and make meaning from unfamiliar words.

- Explain that that the author has used powerful descriptive and expressive words to create an atmosphere in this story. Ask pairs to find examples and to discuss the effect that the language has.